J.B. DANE

RAVEN'S REWARD

Urban Fantasy

A BETWEEN THE BOOKS
RAVEN TALE

3 Media Press

RAVEN'S REWARD

Author's Note: This short novella is

set between

Raven's Moon and *Marked Raven*

in The Raven's Tales series.

Raven's Reward © 2020 Copyright Beth Daniels/ J.B. Dane
ISBN 9798593266675
Published by 3 Media Press, Bardstown, Kentucky

Cover cityscape graphic of Detroit from Dreamstime
Cover design by Beth Daniels

All rights reserved. Except for use in any review, the reproduction or utilization of this work in whole or in part in any form by any electronic, mechanical or other means, now known or hereafter invented, including xerography, photocopying, recording, or file sharing, or in any information storage or retrieval system, is forbidden without written permission from the author. All characters in this book have no existence outside the imagination of the author and have no relation whatsoever to anyone bearing the same name or names. They are not even distantly inspired by any individual known or unknown to the author, and all incidents are pure invention.

THANKSGIVING DAY
and BLACK FRIDAY

Roast turkey was not on the menu my first Thanksgiving Day this side of the fiction line. If the demons, ghouls, trolls, and assorted Otherworldlies gathered on the Amberson Estate had their way, barbecued Raven was in the wind. And all because a damn angel crashed the party.

Not that it was a *party* precisely, though any passersby capable of hearing the racket would think so. It was a yard sale.

I'd swept up the complete households of my most recent victims but as they'd been demons, moving the merchandise on meant no humans were being admitted to the grounds – not even my friendly neighborhood witchy humans or the odd necromancer or stray wizard. The troll guards at the gate had orders not to let anything that had once *been* human in either, which kept the werewolves, zombies, and ghosts away. Sunlight was the vampire deterrent.

Thanksgiving had seemed the appropriate day for the festivities. Not only had research shown me that Thursday was ideal timing for unloading unwanted stuff, but I was going to be damn thankful the junk was off the premises.

Why, you ask?

For one thing, who the heck wants things around that remind that they are the bane of folks who can't help being inhuman? It's not like a being can pick the pool their genes do the hundred-meter butterfly in, right? I oughta know. I'm just passing for human. Still, I'd smote my share of non-humans through twenty volumes of The Raven Tales before turning up in the real world where I'd ended up smiting a few more back around All Hallows. However, the real reason no humans were being admitted was that it was a really bad idea to pass along items tinged with essence of demon to an unsuspecting – or even a suspecting and hopeful – *homo sapien*.

It wasn't on one of Moses's tablets, but there needed to be a commandment that said "Thou shalt not traffic with magic wielding bad dudes shouldst thou not be-eth one thyself."

I sorta was one myself, though I had good intentions. I think we all know that's not a solid recommendation though. Or believable considering I'm on drinking terms with Samael. You know, the guy in the number one spot on the good doers smite list. His rap sheet lists several other names he's called: Lucifer, Old Scratch, Satan...

Not Beelzebub though. That's my trusty dachshundric hellhound's moniker. Mine is Bram Farrell, a.k.a. The Raven, bad ass paranormal P.I. Okay, hopefully *bad ass*.

It was a nearly bucolic setting. The estate upon which I lived, courtesy of my now passed on creator, boasted the sort of acreage dairy cows would appreciate. There were even woodlands within the fenced, gated, and spelled compound. The sun had granted us with an appearance and the folks strolling along the tables of merchandise were diversely not human but leaning toward characters from the Grimm Brothers' collection of tales, so it could be taken for a Ren Faire. But it was a yard sale. For some reason, I had to keep reminding my guests – and I use the term loosely – of that. They were there to fork over cash not devolve into Morris dancing type frolics.

"Nice turn out," a voice said at my shoulder.

Didn't have to turn to identify the speaker. He tended to use aftershave with a hint of sulfur and brimstone in it.

"You come with cash in hand, Sam?"

"Don't be ridiculous, Raven. Did see something I want though," Samael said and indicated what it was with a tip of his chiseled chin.

Naturally, it was the big-ticket item. A really sweet Jeep Wrangler Sahara, dune colored with black removable back cover. Low mileage and ready for off-roading. Even with a forest of pine air fresheners dangling from the rearview mirror, essence of the former demon owner still clung to it.

"You know this sale benefits the families of the Raven Kills," I said. Not that I'd killed the victims in the real world, just in the fictional world where they'd had different names and really deserved what they got. Unfortunately, the Otherworlders of the real world were loath to detach my moniker from the...well, kills.

"Doesn't work that way, Bram. 'Sides, if I hadn't given you that little present, you wouldn't be standing here today," the Devil reminded me.

Oh, yeah. The hellfire that I still could only control in short bursts. I pictured currency sprouting wings and heading out of my grasp.

I sighed, capitulating. Actually, the yard sale was going to net a miniscule amount compared to what was already in the fund. A bit of almost legal prestidigitation had already cleared out bank accounts and sold off property owned by the true miscreants. "I don't have keys for it," I warned him. "Hotwired it for transport."

"Not a problem," he said. The Jeep vanished but Sam didn't.

"You sticking around to shop for the holidays?" I asked.

"Good try at the humor, kid. Fell flat on your face with it though. No, just feel like cruising the tables."

Considering who he was, there was something beyond the Jeep that was calling to him.

Ruth Lund had helped me collect and price things. She's part troll and part dwarf, and, at less than three-foot-tall, suffers from a severe lack of height. Her brother Ralph is part troll and part giant, or a well-fed troll with an extremely overactive pituitary gland. He's massive and the one lacking a personality.

Anyway, there were several items from the confiscated cache that had given her a tingle. That's all she'd tell me. There was something magical about them but what it was was out of her fairytale bound experience. No, Sam had picked up the scent of something. I had a feeling it would be best to keep whatever it was out of his hands.

Yeah, yeah. I know you've probably fallen out of your seat, consumed with laughter over that. Keep something the Devil wants away from him. Ha, ha, pull the other one, Farrell. Allow me to posit this – yep, *posit*. I've lived my entire life in the land where wild thesauruses roam. Could anyone other than The Raven put a crimp in the Light-Bringer's wicket? Yes, I probably strained a metaphor there, but you get the gist.

The fact that Samael was going into hunting dog mode meant I needed to trail at his heels.

"So, you been to Hell lately to see how the minions are doing in the torture fields?" I asked, strolling idly at his side. Had to sidestep a batch of foreshortened troll, elfin, and dwarf offspring engaged in a game of tag with the theophylakto dudes that usually trailed Samael. Not a one was on god guard duty. They were turning tag into something that resembled rugby only without a ball or rules. Beelz had assigned himself as referee, dashing around the running players and barking instructions. Only the theophylakto players appeared to understand hellhoundese but they were ignoring him. And occasionally tripping over the demon dachshund's long black, ground level form.

"Don't need to be there," Sam said. "That's why I created middle management."

I doubt there is a single soul consigned to life in a middle management position anywhere who doesn't believe they are in Hell, so I was copacetic with that.

"Thinking of having an off-season condo or mansion in Detroit and need household goods to furnish it?" I assayed.

He raised a rather aristocratic eyebrow over that. "Considering the city is still scrambling to recover from severe downsizing, some would say there is no difference between some sections of the community and Hell," he said, "So, no. Sticking with Dubai for now. The shopping's better."

Based on how quickly the Jeep had vanished, I rather thought shop*lifting* was more his thing.

"Okay, give me a hint," I pleaded. "What are you looking for? We can arrow in on it if you'd just tell me."

"Will know it if I see it."

Yeah, like I believed an *if* existed. No, it was a *when* he spotted the mystery item that I'd need far more hocus pocus than was currently in my repertoire quiver to keep it out of his hands.

Then I got distracted when Ruth Lund hustled over, gave him a polite nod, tugged on my pant leg, and insisted I was needed at the gate. The vampire minions – those unturned snacks that did daytime errands for their masters – were trying to bull their way past the massive troll bouncers. By the time I got back amidst the buyers, Sam was deep undercover. Normally, he's not as tall as I am so disappearing in the horde was a cinch for him.

Only thing I could do was stroll the pseudo aisles and hope something spoke to me before it whispered to him. Most of the tables were manned – and I use the word loosely – by people Ruth had supplied. There was too much stuff for me to be the only one pushing the merchandise. No one seemed to mind that a rather unwholesome looking ghoul was overseeing kitchen goods. A something-or-other had glamoured itself into a fair estimation of a Hollywood hopeful to push cosmetics, clothing, and costume jewelry. I had already plundered anything made of a precious metal and real gemstones though I hadn't decided what to do with them yet. Not surprising, considering the original owners were demons, there were a lot of torture devices of a kinky bent: handcuffs, whips, cattle prods, and things I preferred not to sully my imagination over the use of. That table was doing a bang-up business.

So was Ralph Lund's food concession. I'd visited the bar and grill he and Ruth ran in the past and found my taste buds would survive longer by not sampling any of the menu items. Particularly not the homebrewed troll beer. But then I was a hard liquor man for the most part, my swilling confined to smooth Evan Williams bourbon.

When a goblin juggling six screaming homunculi dropped one beneath the hooves of a distracted centaur – who wiped the squished remains off its hoof in the grass and continued its interrupted bargaining session – my thoughts turned more and more to the bottle of forgetfulness that awaited me in the study after the close of business.

That's when something dropped from the sky. Something large, glowing, and with feathers.

"I'll take that," the angel said, jerking an item from the hand of a dark elf.

"Don't think so, Raf," Samael snarled, stepping forward to yank the prize from winged-boy's mitt. He was no longer in stealth mode but bulked up to match his opponent. Which meant they were both topping seven foot. Sam had even manifested an admirable span of wings.

"It belongs to Gabriel," the new arrival insisted. It's just a guess, but I figured he was the archangel Raphael. How many feathered dudes answering to Raf could there be?

"Not anymore," the Devil declared.

It was like watching Chris Hemsworth face down Armie Hammer, only no CGI effects were required.

Before the first blow could be thrown – be it via fist or fiery sword – I dashed in, grabbed the damn thing from a distracted Samael's mitt and hightailed it. Beelz looked temporarily stunned as I vaulted over his back. Okay, so it was more like a running step. He plays things fairly close to the ground. But *vault* sounds far more impressive for an action hero, doesn't it? When the hellhound barked at me, the kids leapt to the conclusion that I had entered their game and raced after me, including the theophylaktoses. Probably looked like a sneak thief as I headed for the south lawn trailing a herd of thundering and shouting short things.

Made the mistake of looking back and when I turned it was to hit my face against glistening angel armor. As I bounded off, the item in my hand flew heavenward, just out of everyone's reach. All it would take was one wing stroke to send either of the archangels after it.

It, by the way, belonged in a brass section. Wasn't the sort of instrument one usually associates with the angel Gabriel, who seems more of a trumpet guy. This was a trombone in danger of losing its slide on the tumble back to Earth. Or if it was grabbed at different ends by the determined winged beings.

Sam and Rafael jumped for it at the same time. Think of this as it might happen in slow motion because that is exactly what it looked like to me. Two golden haired giants with massive white wings unfurled, armor twinkling in appreciative sunbeams, the crowd of assorted non-humans all startled enough to stop shopping for five full seconds, and a conglomeration of offspring and theo dudes shouting and leaping about unconcerned with the drama unfolding. The angels rose, they reached . . .

And a sinuous red dragon swooped down out of nowhere, snagged the prize and poofed back out of existence.

You could have heard a pin drop, the sound of the crowd cut off that quickly. Which is saying something considering we were all standing on a carefully tended swathe of grass.

"What was that!" Raphael snarled.

Although I realized he hadn't meant it as a question but more startled exclamation, I answered.

"Looked a lot like a dragon to me." Might have sounded a bit awed. Hadn't thought they were anything more than a fictional melding of damn scary things who fancied human for dinner. At least in the *real* world. We had plenty of them trawling for princesses and jewels and whatever else they might fancy back in fictionland.

"A dragon," Samael repeated. He sounded a bit irritated.

"You on scale rubbing terms with it?" I asked.

The irritated look morphed to one of disgust. Rather than answer, he glared at Raphael. "Tell little brother Gabriel I've got a nice long pitchfork waiting for an introduction to him if he shows his face around here," he growled. By the time Raphael's fist reached Sam's jaw, the Devil had dissolved from the premises. Fortunately, he forewent the echo of evil laughter trailing his departure. In Sam's place, I would have done it. The whole set up screamed for heavy doses of melodrama.

Instead, the Ren Faire . . . er, yard sale, picked up where it had left off. Dragon appearances might have had that ho-hum feel to fairytale folk.

"You!" Raphael snorted, pointing impolitely at me. "How dare a lesser being such as you sully an angelic instrument with your touch."

"My yard sale. My goods. I'm fairly sure you know that horn hasn't been in Heaven for awhile. Also sure that, had you known what had it, one of your choir would have reclaimed it long ago."

"It was among men for a reason," wing boy snarled.

"Yet in demon hands," I pointed out. "Now, you interested in some upscale pots and pans signed by a famous chef or are you leaving?" Might have formed a small ball of fire to toss idly into the air and catch again. The kind that carried the essence of the fiery pit with it. Hellfire is a great deterrent. "We're fresh out of orchestral merchandise."

For an angelic being, his growl sounded a lot like that of a dissatisfied hellhound. Rather than mimic Samael's departure, Raphael let the sweep of his wings handle the dramatics and sailed, with Superman-like speed, into the stratosphere.

I was still staring up at the sky when Beelz joined me, set his haunches down on my foot and stared upwards, too. Ruth Lund trundled over, glanced heavenward, shook her head in disgust, and cleared her throat. I know this because it sounded like she was speaking an Otherworlder language I'd never heard.

Granted, I haven't really *heard* any of them, though it was written that I had and as any being in the magic lexicon knows, words are damn powerful things.

"Pardon?" I said.

"We're going to have to bill that damn dragon for the merchandise," she said. "You want to send one of my cousins with it or take it to his cache yourself?"

Couldn't help it. I stared at her, speechless for . . . well, far longer than anyone who knows me would expect.

"You know the dragon?"

"You mean like personally? Naw. Dragons aren't what you'd call sociable types, though there is one who has a weekly poker game frequented by some of these characters." She waved an arm recklessly to encompass every being in Amberson Field. "He probably knows our shoplifter."

A shoplifting dragon. And people thought things in fictionland were weird. Considering I've long had a reputation for disapproving strongly – as in delivering doses of deadly disapproval – where crime is concerned, policing this snatch and grab was right up my turnpike.

"Ruthie, you wicked darling! Can you get me an invite to this poker game?"

"Naw, Ralph's got a regular chair at the table though. You can go with him. Just take lots of cash," she recommended. "The dragon don't take plastic."

~ ~ ~

The timing for my bill collecting venture worked out well. The card dealing not-so-mythical monster let the chips fall every Friday night. Ralph wasn't thrilled to learn he'd been volunteered to introduce me to the game, but Ruth had her own ways of persuasion. Considering the vast differences in their sizes, I fancied blackmail was her main deterrent. Made one wonder what sort of skeletons Ralph feared falling from his closet. Could have been real skeletons with toothmarks marring them. That would certainly serve as evidence for the prosecution.

The card dealing dragon answered to the inconceivable name of Bub. Whether it was short for something or not, I didn't need to know. The game was held in a dilapidated and sensibly abandoned deathtrap of a warehouse. We have a lot of these in Detroit but, considering the size of our host, the building served well. If his tail twitched in the wrong direction and took out support pillars it would only matter if the roof fell in on we more fragile beings.

Bub was a rather common dragon, big and bulky. The couch potato version. He was also green. No imagination in that. Considering he wore a dealer's visor over his eyes, which was also green, though a different shade, and managed to hold regular sized cards in his claws, the only things scary about the dude were his size and the grate of his voice.

"Raven," he rumbled, sounding like gravel was being ground down to pebble size. Maybe he was multi-tasking? "Never heard ya were a gambler afore."

I wasn't. Not where money was concerned, that is. Considering all the close calls I'd had survival-wise through twenty books and the touch-and-go ones in the real world a couple weeks back, I was an X-treme risk taker.

"Expanding my interests," I said while taking temptation from my inner jacket pocket and tapping the two-inch tall stack of twenties on the table, aligning them neatly. "We use chips here or just toss cash on the table?"

"Chips is a waste of time," another of the players spat. Fortunately, though he looked like a being capable of generating acidic saliva, the table didn't gain further personality due to a toxically hungry bit of drool. The claw scratches across the surface sufficed as enhancement.

"Game's five-card draw," Bub announced. "I don't toss any of youse a card 'til I see the color of yer cash and a C-note's worth in the pot. None better be that vanishing gold this time, O'Clankahan," he snarled at a leprechaun perched on a stack of ancient encyclopedias.

"I ain't no bamboozler," the little man snarled and pushed the sleeves of a generic gray hoodie up. "See, no cards up me sleeve either ya big bag o' gas." The blue pompom on his Detroit Lion's knit cap bobbed as he leaned forward to toss his contribution into the center of the table. The hundred was pristine enough to have just come off the printing press.

Apparently satisfied, the dragon turned his gaze on each of his other guests in turn. We anteed up quickly.

I scooped up the cards he sailed my way. Arranging them in my hand didn't matter. It was a hand worthy of zip consideration. "I was sorta hoping to run into one of your brothers tonight, Bub. Just saw him in passing yesterday. Blood red fella with midnight highlights and some Celestial ancestry, though not a purebred. Didn't catch his name."

The green dragon pinned me with a suspicious amber gaze. "What's yer interest in him, Farrell?"

I tapped my cards together, tucking them face down on the tabletop. "His visit was brief, but he left with something of mine. I'd like it back."

Mein host turned his attention back to the cards in his claws. "Wouldn't have been a horn by any chance."

"Might have been," I allowed.

Bub sighed. "The Collector. That lizard is nuts about brass instruments. He's got a jazz club and a pet band to serenade him every night. If you're smart, you'll forget about that horn. He's in tight with the vampire mafia."

"The ones with offices at One Detroit Center?" I'd had a run in with them not long ago.

"Thems the ones," he said. "Now, I got a question fer ya."

"Wouldn't be do I have a death wish, would it?" I asked.

"I read them books, Raven. I know ya do. What I wanta know is how many new cards ya need?"

Five would have been nice. I asked for four.

And the name of the red dragon's jazz club.

RAVEN'S REWARD

SATURDAY

Fairy tale types have got no imagination. The troll siblings call their bar The Bridge. The horn thief called his club The Red Dragon. Still, it was a couple steps up from the taverns I'd patronized back in fictionland. The patrons shunned jeans and t-shirts, going for upscale suits and cocktail dresses. You could order comestibles from a Szechuan or Cajun menu. The recorded musical palate leaking through hidden speakers harkened decades back as did the décor and the Playboy bunny style getups of the wait girls. Sinatra would have felt right at home.

The dragon looked a lot different than the last time I'd seen him. He'd glamoured down to human form and shoved it into a dark suit he might have stolen from a yard sale at Cary Grant's house around the middle of the 20th century.

I wasn't the only one who'd tracked him down though. Spotted Samael in the back, the flickering candle inside a red cylinder on the table highlighting his sinister expression. He probably knew I'd put in an appearance, but he only had eyes for brother Raphael. That troublesome archangel was holding down a horseshoe shaped booth on the opposite side of the room. He appeared to have brought a date, a tasty looking cookie in a short sparkly dress with a spectacular amount of dusky skin on display. Both angelic bros were in mock human form, though for their build and get ups they'd taken cues from both romance covers and ads in GQ when they morphed to lesser being status. Had gone with suits from Dolce & Gabbana. Well, I had, too. Sometimes a guy must up his sartorial elegance to blend in.

It being a holiday weekend, the joint was packed with regular folks out for a good time. Having come stag, I snagged a stool at the bar and ordered my preferred poison. A double.

Had spent my day doing a bit of research. Let's face it, with so many contenders interested in it, the horn had to have one heck of a history. I needed to know if it was a lethal one. It's always good to be prepared for curses or plagues of locust and similar things.

All I'd come up with was info on trumpets, but that didn't discourage me. I come from a land where imagination trumps reality. To fit what was required, a trumpet could morph into a complete oompah band.

From what I discovered, the snagged trombone likely had a spectacular past in a different shape, one that started with Joshua spitting into its mouthpiece to rubble-ize the walls of Jericho. There was a good chance Gabriel had lent it to him or been given a direct order to hand it over for the Higher One's purposes.

As the Medieval Period oozed into the Renaissance, enterprising troubadour suppliers tinkered the basic trumpet into something that would sound a bit different. Painters liked the curves the new instrument sported and began incorporating it into sacred paintings, putting it in the hands of that angelic horde, which is likely when Gabe's cornet decided to upgrade itself. No one seemed to mind that the creators had failed to come up with a good merchandising name for their product. I mean, they called the damn thing a "sackbut". Who the hell wants to play something with that sort of name?

The answer is musicians who don't care what something's called as long as the sound it makes gives them tingles. Wasn't long before folks began associating the sonorous sound of these infant trombones with death and what comes after.

You've got to admit, that sort of a rep tends to let thoughts sprint off at a mad gallop toward the Apocalypse.

Considering I'd only been on this side of the book binding for a few short weeks, the idea that a horn capable of kicking off the End of Days was being warred over by beings who weren't human — which might mean they wouldn't be affected in the least by Doomsday — didn't sit well with me.

But which team did I want to have snag this thing in the end? *I* sure the hell didn't want to be the keeper of a thing capable of sacking mankind's butt.

I might be one of Samael's drinking buddies occasionally — not like I have an option when he turns up — but that didn't mean I'd trust him with the horn. Raphael hadn't impressed me as worthy either. Couldn't help wondering why Gabriel hadn't come to claim his property personally. Why send his jerk brother?

There was nothing to do but await developments. I sipped EW, killing time before the band took the stand.

Naturally, that's when the vampire contingent showed up. At least it wasn't the lower caste snacks but the upper echelon this time 'round. There were five in all. Renaissance Dude, Miss Sweden 1934, Surfer Boy Yves, and two svelte dudes who might have been off-duty men's cologne models, though ones who didn't work daylight hours. I'd met the first three. They hadn't given me their names, though the godfather of the bunch had called Yves by name back then.

They slid past me without a greeting but that didn't get me off the hook. They'd barely settled at a table near the token dance floor when one of the Bunnies slid her red lacquered digits along my arm. "Mr. Farrell?" she queried softly. "Mr. Palermo would like you to join his party."

"Palermo? 'Faid I don't know anyone by that name, sugar," I said.

It wasn't going to get me out of the invite though for she leaned against my shoulder, her head tilted toward mine and directed my gaze back across the room. "The gentleman at the table with the woman in the red dress, sir."

"Oh. Him," I groaned. "He didn't happen to say what it was about?"

"No, sir," she murmured, the patented polite smile of wait staff the world over curving her pretty lips, then she moved on to collect drink orders from other patrons.

I tossed off the remainder of bourbon in my glass for a modicum of false courage and ambled through the crowd to Renaissance Palermo's table. Considering I'd been invited over, no one smiled when I arrived.

The don gestured to a different bunny girl and requested that I receive a refill on the liquified corn.

"No need. I'm not staying to chat," I told her.

"Yes, you are," Palermo said. Yves kicked a chair out, either attempting to bruise my shins or offer a seat.

"Has everyone eaten today?" I asked. Let's face it. Vampires only drink alcoholic beverages to blend in, not to wash down chicken fingers. Wanted to make sure sautéed wing of Raven in a nice Type AB sauce wasn't on the menu.

"Sit," Palermo ordered rather than clarify dinner arrangements.

I sat.

"Don't interfere," he said.

"With...?"

"My associate."

"The dragon? He stole property that was for sale, you know. Not in the least bit polite."

Considering the archangels had tried the snatch and fly themselves, there was a massive outbreak of sticky fingers abroad.

"Name the amount, and it will be paid," Palermo said.

Oh, sure. Like that was going to happen. If I'd guessed right, chances were blowing even a lone off-key note on the horn would decimate the rock we all called home.

I leaned back in my chair. "Sorry, but there has been considerable interest in the instrument in question and the price just keeps going up and up." In fact, it was now so high it was priceless and off the market until I figured out where Mount Doom was and could toss the damn thing in after Frodo's nasty little ring.

"And yet you don't have it in your possession," old Renaissance reminded, "which should make it difficult to sell."

Kinda thought it had always been difficult to sell, at least legally, considering what I surmised it could do. It had terrorist feature of the month written all over it.

Of course, I hadn't exactly come into possession of it legally either. I'd just helped myself to everything in sight, emptying a kaput demon's habitat.

"Possession's nine-tenths of the law," Yves said.

I glanced over at him. "Does the court system know that?"

"The topic is whether you do or don't have title to the item in question, Raven," Miss Sweden said. "Considering our host is in possession of it, you would have difficulty proving ownership. Unless you have a receipt for its purchase?"

"I have something better," I said. "I have witnesses who saw said flying red lizard snatch the horn. In fact, two of them are here with us tonight. A couple of angelics."

Having felt Sam's and Raf's glares burning laser-like into my back as I crossed the room to the vamp table, I knew dangerous backup was at hand. I'm being factious in even considering either of the Heaven spat brothers *backup*, naturally. They were both there to snag the trombone themselves.

Nobody was interested in paying for it. Not even me since there was a good chance the price tag read "One soul." If I had one, it was barely used. I wanted more mileage out of it.

"Name a price, Farrell. The longer you delay, the less likely I am to ensure that any payment is given," Palermo said.

Right. Of all the beings interested in the instrument, he was the least dangerous of the contenders. He'd been human once. The Apocalypse wasn't going to treat him kindly. The dragon had probably immigrated in from another dimension and could blink back to it if Earth blew. The angels would simply return to their designated corners of the universe. Mankind, on the other hand, would be screwed.

"Not talking to any middleman on this," I announced and stood up. "This is between me and The Collector."

"Then you'll fail on both counts," the vamp said. "Retrieval of the item is not in your power and payment will not be forthcoming."

"Still haven't read any of my adventures, have you." I wasn't making a query. If he had read any of the Raven Tales, he wouldn't have tossed down a gauntlet. There was nothing like telling me something was impossible to make me decide proving the opposite was a damn good idea. Even if it nearly killed me. *Nearly* being the operative word.

"My senses tell me you are posing as a viable meal receptacle, Farrell, not that you are one. Your scent is still strongly of wood pulp, not plasma, and wood is extremely susceptible to flames," he goaded.

I didn't need the reminder that graduating from Pinocchio to human was still on my bucket list. The chip on my shoulder leaned toward hawthorn, which means I have a slow burn with good heat output, be it regular fire or the upgrade to hellfire. However, when last we'd rumbled, I'd been languishing in the magic department. He probably didn't know my hocus-pocus was powering up. Not that everything I'd once done in a book was online yet, but I had high retrieval hopes.

"Then we have that in common, don't we?" I essayed. "Your kind burns rather spectacularly when lit up, too. I'm sure the dragon would be glad to torch either of us. He'd consider it pest control."

Somewhere off stage a figurative cookie timer chimed to let the band know they were on the clock. There wasn't a curtain that closed, just a backdrop swathe with the club's logo emblazoned on it, a flame tinged red caligraphied dragon on a modest blanket of onyx. The first man to settle on the raised platform was the drummer, twin sets of sticks and whisk brushes in hand. A bass fiddle player followed him then the ivory tickler arrived. The last man on stage had – much to my relief – a saxophone, rather than a trombone, slung around his neck on a red cord.

I turned my back on the vampires, fairly sure that in a room full of normal humans that one wouldn't pounce on me. But one did pounce. The hand on my arm had the strength of an Olympic bench presser behind it. A glance down showed that the fingers curled around my jacket sleeve were pale, long, and shaped to a nice black lacquered point. The vampiress's smile probably looked pleasant to those at the tables around us but I was reading an entirely different message in her eyes. Considering she'd shrugged off the draped thingy she'd come in the door wearing, I noted that the designer of her dress had favored conservation of fabric when constructing the top part and used soft, clinging fabric at that.

"Dance with me, Raven," Ingrid purred. Not that her name was Ingrid, but as a tall, slinky, blue-eyed blonde, she was working a Nordic vibe. "You do know how to dance, don't you?"

Honestly, I didn't know whether I could or not. Had danced out of range of allocamuli spit balls and to avoid counter curses a few times in fictionland but I wasn't up to Maksim Chmerkoskiy standards. However, as my creator had spent years attending functions where the wealthy cut light fantastics as they schmoozed, was pretty sure I had the basics to even pull off a decent tango.

When I didn't answer immediately, the well-preserved Jessica Rabbit knockoff let her grin turn mocking. "Afraid I'll bite you?"

"Maybe," I conceded, but I did put my arm around her as the band moved into their first number. My hand touched warm bare skin. A wide expanse of it. At least temperature-wise, it appeared she'd popped someone's handy vein the moment she rolled out of her coffin at sundown. Although there was enough blood in my system to leak out when I got injured, it didn't seem to be worth noshing on. Of course, maybe they were saving me for later.

The musicians were competent though not of a quality to cause David Sanborn's team to lose sleep over them. I didn't recognize the song, but dancing depends more on the beat and the way the drummer was brushing the skins said slow and easy. Encouraged that they wouldn't be the first to take to the floor, two other couples joined us.

"So why exactly are we dancing? You have secrets to pass along?" I asked falling into a lazy fox trot. Not ballroom competition level but at least she let me lead.

Blondie smirked. "Secrets?"

"Hell, I'll take double crosses as long as I'm not the one being double crossed, sweetheart," I said.

Heidi's laugh was low and throaty. Sorta the way you'd expect a femme fatale with blood thirst to sound. "Raven," she chided. "I merely do as I'm told. I've no intention of going against Mr. Palermo's wishes."

We did a couple quick steps in sync. "So he wanted to know if I had social skills," I mused guiding her into a modest underarm spin. The skirt of her scarlet dress spun a bit, too, as she moved back into my arms.

"Let's say you have both surprised and disappointed him in the past," she countered.

"Disappointed him?" Hell! Couldn't have that now, could we? "How did I manage that? By surviving our previous meeting?"

She shrugged, an action that displaced red silk in interesting ways. "Possibly it was the low company you kept."

"I was new in town, honey," I said, though the folks I mingled with back in fictional Detroit were of the same frequently degenerate species that I'd met in *real* Detroit.

"True," she conceded, "but you aren't quite what we expected."

Oddly enough, my creator had felt that way, too.

"Tonight, he simply wanted you far from your angelic cohorts," she added.

That didn't sound good.

It's also when I realized that she'd herded me toward a service door at the back of the room. A massive bouncer stepped forth. His hand landed solidly on my shoulder. Freyja swiveled into a waiting Yves's arms and glided away.

"Ya wanta talk ta the dragon?" the muscle growled. "Well, the dragon wants ta talk ta ya, Farrell."

I'm not all that sure that my feet were involved in the transfer to the alley behind the club, but that's where we headed.

~ ~ ~

It was narrow, filthy, but bright out back. A security bulb beamed super nova light on the scene. Okay, so maybe it was just having it blinding me that made it feel like that. Both my cretin escort and the glamoured dragon had their backs to it. I was holding down the role of bug on an entomologist's specimen board, the goon's forearm pressed against my throat, securing me to a grimy brick wall, my feet resting on nothing more solid than the breeze.

Because I have a reputation that leans toward stupidity, I stared into the dragon's canted amber orbs. "I came to reclaim the horn," I croaked beyond the strangle hold.

He snorted at the idea. Tendrils of smoke drifted into obscurity between us. He tilted his human-like snout, giving the minion a silent order. I crashed to the alley floor.

"Reclaim? I dragged you out here to demand it back," he said.

"If you'd bothered to pay for –" I snarled, climbing to my feet. That's when my mind caught up to the conversation. "Wait. You don't have it?"

"I. Don't. Have. It." That sounded pretty emphatic.

"You left it unattended?" I was flabbergasted over such a possibility.

"I put it in my safe," he said. "It's not there now but you've been lurking about."

I'd been sitting at the bar in clear sight until the vamp invite shifted me to a table and then the dance floor.

"Hand it over," he demanded.

I echoed his own words. "I. Don't. Have. It. Hell, it's impossible to hide a trombone either in a pocket or up a sleeve."

He tapped a finger against his chin in mock thought. "Let's see. Magic horn. Magic wielder. Yeah, I think it's very possible for you to have it on your person, Farrell. Search him."

Considering there was nothing to find, we were all left empty handed, though I was the only one feeling bruised as well.

"I want that horn," the dragon snarled and yanked the rear door open.

"So do a lot of others," I snapped. The door slammed behind him and the bouncer, the sound as emphatic as rulebound punctuation.

Alone in the security spotlight, I dusted soot from my sleeve and wondered who'd nabbed the trombone from the trombone nabber.

Then the vampires pushed into the night and I went bug status again.

Yves had brought the cologne dudes with him. Each of them grabbed a shoulder and squished me into the masonry. "Who'd you hire to steal the horn, Farrell?" the mock surfer demanded.

"Have any of you morons ever opened a friggin' book? Twenty volumes, dude, and in each one I work alone. The system works. Why would I change it?"

"Because you think we'd expect you to do the job alone and decided a distraction would work better," he bitched.

"Well, it would if I thought the way you do, but I don't, fang boy," I snarled.

The helper vamps eased their grip enough to put space between my back and the wall, then slammed me back so fast, my head attempted a bank shot off the brick.

"Where are you accepting delivery of it?" Yves growled.

"Do you have the least idea of what the damn thing could, would, or will do?" I barked.

He shrugged. "Not my department. I'm only here to beat an answer out of you."

"I already gave you my answer," I said. "Don't have it. Don't know who does." Wished I didn't care who had it, but I did. There were too many dangerous hands the horn could fall into.

Yves's fist didn't accept my answer. He put a good bit of vampiric anger into the blow, a solar plexus punch like the one that killed Houdini. I slumped to the ground when his associates released me. Not satisfied that I hurt enough, though I was fairly sure that I did, one of them kicked me in the ribs.

"Let's try this one more time," Yves suggested once I managed to breathe again.

I made a counteroffer and added an incentive. "Let's not," I gasped as I flicked sulfur infused flames toward the cologne boys' trouser legs. If you've read one of the Raven Tales, you know I have no problem ridding the world of their sort. They flamed up nicely on either side of me. I blipped a shield in place to keep vamp ashes off my suit.

Yves stumbled back so quickly, he smashed up against the opposite wall and jostled the giant Dumpster. A moment later, he'd left the scene.

The twin undead torches went their holocaustal way in quick order, leaving nothing more than a couple burn marks on the asphalt and the echoes of some rather girlish screams bouncing off the alley walls. By the time I was able to sit up, even the scent of hellfire had dissipated.

Or I thought it had.

When Raphael came through the door, he flinched and held his arm up to his face, as though he could block a foul scent. Samael was right behind him. The Devil grinned when he caught the faint remaining aroma.

Raphael rounded on him. "You gave him that?"

Sam shrugged. "He's amusing. Whadda toast, kid?"

I sat where I was, forearms resting on raised knees. "Nobody you knew," I said. "Don't tell me you think I've got that damn horn, too."

Sam smirked. "We're higher beings, Bram. We can tell it's not on the premises."

"So where is it?" I asked.

"That's what I want to know," Raphael snapped.

"There's something I want to know, too," I said. "What the hell are each of you planning to do with that damn trombone if you get your hands on it?"

"Return it to its proper owner," Raf declared. He sounded all holier than thou batshit crazy rather than honest though.

"And that would be Gabriel?" I queried.

There was a telling pause before he said, "Yes. Who else?"

"You used to be a better liar," Sam told him. "Out of practice?"

"What about you, Sam?" I demanded.

"Balancing the odds, are you, kid?" he drawled, arms folded across his chest, a shoulder propped against the building. "I'd cache it for use at a far more auspicious time."

"I'll bet that when the horn gets blown, the halls of Hell will be filled to capacity." Overcrowding in the Afterlife would make a lot of city dwelling souls feel right at home, wouldn't it?

"Something like that," he agreed.

"Which is likely to happen when?" I pushed.

"Eons from now," he said. "There's still plenty of hell space in this dimension to expand into."

That sounded like a good option except the Prince of Liars had given it. I wasn't about to put money down on that Brooklyn Bridge.

Brushing my hands together, I got to my feet rather than loll at the highly buffed brogue covered feet of the celestial beings. In their current forms, neither quite matched me in height.

That didn't stop Raphael from making a move on me. I'd expected it though. Arch-boy had already demonstrated a severe lack of temper control. When the ball of hellfire bloomed between us, Sam chuckled but Raf flinched away.

"I don't have the frickin' horn. I don't know who does or where it is," I said. "But I'll find it. It's what I do."

Sam gestured to me with a thumb. "It is what he does," he told Raphael.

Raf didn't look convinced. Guess there was no lending library beyond the Golden Gates, not that he seemed like a reader type. "And when you do," he snarled, "who gets it?"

Although they were smudged by unknown alley elements, I shot my cuffs. Straightened my tie. Ran my fingers back through well tousled hair. "Honestly? No idea," I admitted and strolled back to my car.

~ ~ ~

It was still early when I got home. Beelz was waiting up for me. I stripped off my now less than perfect jacket, tossed the tie after it, and took a seat on the kitchen floor next to him. I'd swung by a fast food place to acquire a picnic dinner for the two of us. He nosed the bun open on his sandwich and settled in to enjoy his burger. I did nothing more creative than rearrange the bacon slices on my double before digging in. His had already disappeared by then.

"If you acquired a hot piece of merchandise, where would you hide it?" I asked him between bites.

The demonic dachshund gave it some consideration then got to his feet, trundled over to his doggie bed, and went to work digging at the collection of towels he used in place of sheets.

"Bury it, hmm? Not a bad idea. But where?"

He returned to where I was stretched out, my back against a lower cupboard, dropped belly down on the tile and rested his muzzle on my ankles. It was his favorite stance for pondering.

"It's not like either the vampires or the dragon have nice large yards like we do. These blood suckers don't even hang out in forgotten mausoleums. And, before you suggest it, the dragon's got a safe rather than a treasure cave."

Beelz made a disgruntled nose. I knew how he felt.

We were no closer to an answer by the time I'd popped the final french fry.

Sometimes doing something mindless allows the mind to scramble the facts already gathered in a case and put them together in new and interesting configurations. I amscrayed to the front parlor. In the weeks since Beelz and I'd become the sole residents of the mansion, it had been transformed into a media room. No more 24-inch screen for me, which is the size of the one that decorated my bedroom in the past. I'd upgraded to a 110-inch monster and had speakers arranged for surround sound. It was great for catching up on all the movies and television shows I'd been quoting lines from for years without ever having seen them. The evening news, though? Well, that made me wish I hadn't passed the smaller screen on to a charity shop. No one needs to see the ongoing destruction of the world by politicians, criminals, and folks with hyperactive fanatic glands in supersized detail.

Still, I headed to the media room, grabbed the remote, flicked the news on, and collapsed on the sofa. Beelz followed me but curled up for an after-dinner snooze beneath the padded and tuffed leather coffee table. I put a large toss pillow over my face to block the real-world atrocities from sight.

Although Black Friday had passed, the lead stories were still about violence perpetrated by insane bargain shoppers. No one had been killed but injuries and arrests had continued into the weekend. An overly perky female voice threatened viewers with the weather forecast. A guy talking gibberish in a rapid-fire delivery brought me up to par on sporting news.

And then, in a reversal of doom and gloom, an on-the-scene junior reporter related a miracle.

A mob scene had been building at one of the local warehouse sized stores. Far more customers had come to both stretch their budget and make a kid ecstatic for five minutes by purchasing the season's fastest selling movie tie-in toy. Supplies were limited and, even though management had held the item back to use as a dinner-time door buster feature, more than twice the number of expected rabid buyers had turned up to claim one. Store security guards were in danger of being hospitalized when furious shoppers began attacking with weighted purses, sports equipment, and hurled cans from the grocery section.

Then, the reporter said, the sound of a harmonica playing a holiday song crept through the store and the warrior shoppers' berserker mood changed. Peace began settling over the battle floor. A few apologies were made. Several people who had been in slayer mode moments earlier remembered they were healthcare professionals and began attending to the injured.

I tossed the pillow and swung my feet back to the floor. Upped the volume on the set. Beelz raised his head and focused on the giant screen, too.

The man standing next to the reporter had the sort of face it was easy to forget. His clothing wasn't remarkable either. Behind him was the banner and kettle of The Salvation Army.

"It was wild," he said into the hand-held microphone the news person had shoved before him. "I was actually thinking it would be a good idea to make tracks, so I didn't land in the middle of the crowd."

"Had you been playing the harmonica prior to this?" the reporter asked.

The guy shook his head. "Nope. Don't own one. Fact is, even if I had one, I wouldn't have thought playing it was a good idea at the time. People were streaming past me out of the store to avoid the fight. The only reason I didn't join them is that if the mob knocked the drum over...well, there would have been a second mad rush as folks scooped up the spilled cash.

"Then this man asked me if I knew how to play a harmonica. Well, I can, not well, but folks usually recognize what I'm playing. He suggested 'The Christmas Song'. Nice and non-denominational, he said." The charity volunteer chuckled. "He even said he'd stand by to protect the kettle while I played. I thought he was nuts. Know what he said? 'Music sooths the savage soul.' Weird that it did, huh?"

Very weird I thought.

Also wondered whether I'd been totally wrong about what the missing trombone's purpose was. Could there be two magical instruments aboard in Detroit this holiday season, one delivering peace and one delivering the opposite? Somehow, it seemed unlikely.

But if an apocalyptic trumpet transmuted into a trombone, why couldn't a trombone change its affiliation and morph into an easily carried, easily concealed harmonica that promoted good will?

I had an entirely new direction to head and more questions to answer.

Who had access to the red dragon's safe headed the list. The latest nabbing had to be an inside job.

Who – or even what – was the guy manning the contribution kettle and how had he happened to volunteer this year? Had he received a celestially whispered suggestion that led him to donate his time?

Who was the good Samaritan with a harmonica conveniently stashed in his pocket, and why had he thought it would calm the maddening crowd?

There was nothing much I could do yet that night, but there was one question that I could get answered. I called Ruth Lund at The Bridge.

It sounded like there was a holiday riot in progress at the bar, but that merely meant the usual customers were being their usual non-charming selves.

"You want to know what?" Ruth shouted over the racket.

"Which of our demons had a trombone among the items you packed?" I yelled back so she could hear me.

"A trombone? You mean the one the dragon stole?"

"Yeah."

"I thought you'd found it in the attic at your place and added it to the sale," she said, "'cause it sure wasn't something any of those demons owned."

SUNDAY

When Sunday dawned, I'd not only sorted out who I needed to see, what to ask them, and watched all four *Men in Black* movies, donuts had been consumed. There isn't much a guy can do in the investigation biz when most of the folks he needs to talk to are sleeping. Sleep apparently isn't something I do. Never was mentioned that I did it in a book, and that seems to be holding true in the real world, too. If I ever do discover a need to sleep, I'll use that as the sign that I finally am human. In the meantime, Beelz enjoys nice snoozes; I do nightly movie marathons.

Granted, I could have taken a middle of the night stumble into the estate's wooded area to make an appointment with Sam. As there was a definite chance of breaking my leg in the dark, I put it off. Besides, the theophylaktoses probably weren't sleeping either but they'd really decide I was trying to take out their boss after usual business hours if I tripped over one of them. Waiting until first light worked best. They'd see me coming and let the Devil know I wanted a chat. You'd think appointments could be made through Beelz considering he hailed from Hell, but apparently it doesn't work that way. The theos handle secretarial appointments as well as rain on visitors from the trees.

When it was light enough to trawl through said trees toward where the enchanted meadow poofs into being, I wasn't surprised when the first little dude splatted at my feet. Three of his pals bounced off the invisible shield I'd raised, two landing in brambles, the third doing damage to an oak sapling.

"No fair!" one of the bramble bound beings yelled.

"Considering by now you should know that your lord has nothing to fear from me —" Like he feared anything, right? "—I'd hoped these asinine attacks would cease," I snapped and dropped the shield.

I'm not sure what theophylaktoses are other than short, not naturally occurring among Earth's many species, and dimwitted, but they are seriously loyal. To Sam they are the equivalent of court jesters. They just don't know it.

The one that had gone splat on the path pushed to his feet. "You are a witch's golem and thus . . ." His voice trailed off as he noticed I was carrying something. "What's in the bag?"

"Donuts with sprinkles."

"And lemon cream filling?" another of my attackers asked hopefully.

"Naturally," I assured and tossed the bag to him. "Boss available for a chat?"

As all four of them had their mouths stuffed, they nodded in unison and pointed toward the meadow. Sam had brought the iron patio chairs with the flame stitched cushions. On the table between them sat tall capped cups with the Starbucks' logo imprinted on the side.

"Odd how you always know when I'll be along," I said, taking a seat and helping myself to a cup of so-not-joe.

"You're predictable," the Devil said.

"I'm predictable?"

"You got tells, kid. They were spilling off you last night when you walked out of that alley. What I'm interested in is how they involve me."

"They don't really," I admitted. "You didn't know that it was that trombone that was giving you vibes at the yard sale, but Raphael knew it was there and so did the dragon. I need to know how they both learned about it. The dragon I can find. Arch-boy not so much. You know how I can get in touch with him?"

There was a smirk riding Samael's lips when he answered. "Prayer?"

I did a taste test on the coffee. It was putting off enough heat, the Starbucks he'd patronized had probably been the one at Third and Main in the center of Hell. "I haven't heard that that guarantees immediate answers," I said. "There a time gap or does everything run through Michael's black ops group before being passed along?"

Sam stretched his legs out. Crossed his ankles, knitted his fingers together and let them rest in the center of his chest. He was doing a casual day, but a designer one. His jeans showed wear and tear, but they'd come off the production line with that look. He'd gone with my usual choice of black t-shirt and was trying for the common man look with a gray hoodie over it. I was still clinging to the now much the worse for wear Diesel Wieter black leather jacket I'd been wearing upon my arrival from fictionland in October.

"It's been a really long time since I was on that side of the gate, Bram," he reminded. "There weren't as many prayers being shuttled into the mail slots in those days. No saints needed to pick up the slack yet. Still, it depended on who was making the call on whether there was an immediate response. A few of the Old Man's pets got personal visits back then, too."

"Abraham, Moses, Noah?" I asked for clarification's sake.

"A few other prophets, too."

"This is a long-winded shrug you're giving me," I pointed out.

"Yep."

"Just need Raphael's direct dial number," I said.

"It's Sunday, kid. Just go to church," Sam suggested.

"Which church?"

But he was gone. Not even a lingering Cheshire cat smile left hanging the air. He'd also taken the coffee with him. Before I could move, the patio furniture poofed. I hit the ground.

Rather than scramble back up, I enjoyed the way the sky moved from a rosy glow to blue, then dug my cell out. I'd upgraded since All Hallows so I now had all the bells and whistles available. A couple touches to the screen and I was on the Web and scrolling through the Detroit Yellow Pages.

~ ~ ~

Couldn't help but wonder whether the Archdiocese of Detroit was responsible for Raphael's far from angelic attitude. Both he and St. Dunstan had lost out to St. Thomas the Apostle when attendance drops coincided with a scarcity of priests. This resulted in the merging of parishes in 2014. Apparently, it was who you knew, and an Apostle topped an archangel on this game board. St. Dunstan hadn't built a promotion platform on social media, so he was headed in the same direction as St. Romaric. In other words, soon to be forgotten by everyone but church historians.

Well, I'd remember Romaric. I'd nearly turned up my toes in the cemetery of his now vanished church at the cusp of the month.

But Raphael? He's one of the few angels awarded a name in the Torah, the Old Testament, and the Koran. You'd think he'd rate higher than an apostle. Which was probably why he was ticked off. From what I read online after finding the address of the church, he was supposedly a healer, a destroyer of demons, and despised his satanic brother. Well, one out of three ain't bad. He definitely gave off vibes on that last one.

Since Raf no longer merited a church of his own, I headed to St. Thomas's on the off chance that he visited. Could be one of his previous parishioners remembered he'd still be listening and would help them jump the line for an answer. The church was in Garden City, which is west of Dearborn, which is west of downtown Detroit. Not far as a raven flies, but I've never had wings, so I drove. At least traffic on Sunday morning is fairly light.

My timing was perfect. Worshippers from the early service were streaming from the parking lot and it was still too early for the next batch to arrive. If Raf was going to answer my prayer – which was going to sound far more like an interrogation – we wouldn't be interrupted.

I slipped in the door and imitated a tourist at the Vatican, strolling down the aisles and admiring the fixtures. Ushers were still on duty, but a nod and a vague smile satisfied them. I glanced at my watch as though checking how long there was until the next service. Took a seat on the side aisle halfway to the altar.

"Calling the archangel Raphael in reference to a trombone he is interested in," I said beneath my breath.

I don't know if others could see him but he poofed into the pew ahead of me and twisted, his arm along the back of the seat, the better to glare at me. He'd gotten hold of an old romance cover since last night, the kind that still included heads on the models. He looked more like a golden-haired Fabio, though he was wearing a suit and tie rather than have his chest in view.

"You've found it?" he snarled.

"Still looking, but it would help if you'd tell me how you knew it was among the items at my yard sale. Sam didn't know about it ahead of time. He just sensed something out-of-the-ordinary was there. You, on the other hand, went right to it."

He drummed his fingers. I hoped that indicated he was thinking. One never knows with angelics. Not that I've trafficked with many of them, still . . .

"I noticed it was missing from Gabe's collection, so I started asking around to see if he'd lent it out to someone," Raphael said.

"Someone. Another angel? A saint?" I asked.

"He hangs out with Miller, Holly, Lennon and some other musicians so there was a chance that he simply left it in their rehearsal hall after sitting in for a jam session," Raf explained. "While coaxing a tune from it down here might be disastrous, it's harmless near the Gates."

"Glenn Miller, Buddy Holly and John Lennon are all in Heaven?" I would have guessed Händel, Verdi, Bach, Chopin – those kinds of guys, not 20th century rock and swing dudes.

Arch-boy frowned at me. "There's a lot of space on the Plains of Purgatory outside the Gates, Farrell. Cities upon cities of folks waiting to be processed. Those of us who live inside do stroll out to hobnob, and Gabe can't resist making a glorious noise."

Didn't sound like this angel was a music lover. Maybe he thought Gabriel had gone native around the human souls.

"So how did you find out the horn was on Earth?" I was also curious about that cryptic comment he'd made at the yard sale about it being on the planet for a reason. If not to blow the place to smithereens, what reason could there be?

"Grapevine. I know a guy who knows a guy who . . ."

I held my hand up. "I get the drift. So, who was the guy last in line, the one who actually saw the horn in my yard?"

Raf shook his head. "No idea. I just know the person who talked to me."

"Talked to you? As in they sent a prayer your way or do you have a regular route you visit down here?"

He looked confused.

"Dude. You're supposedly a healer. I thought maybe you made the rounds of hospital wards, nursing homes, that sort of thing."

The angel took a deep breath. Let it out slowly. "Okay, it's this way," he said. "I was visiting the sick. The mentally ill. Or at least those that others consider mentally ill. My contact isn't nuts, merely gifted."

"Gifted," I repeated. Had a feeling the answer wasn't going to be all that helpful.

"She sees things."

"A mystic? A psychic?"

"A witch," he said.

RAVEN'S REWARD

~ ~ ~

Fortunately for me, Raf wasn't bound by legal gibberish that disallowed him supplying a patient's name and address. He even had a phone number I could call. Unfortunately, when I called it, no one answered. He figured they were at church. That meant I had more time to kill.

The Red Dragon wasn't open for business yet, but the door was unlocked as employees drifted in. The dragon himself was behind the bar. He wasn't drinking coffee or orange juice but something that looked suspiciously like a Bloody Mary. At least, that's what I hoped it was rather than blood from a human Mary.

"You found the horn?" he demanded.

"Nope, but I'm tracking it," I assured him. "And in the interests of clearing this up quickly, I need some information from you."

He downed his drink for fortification and refilled it. I was relieved to see tomato juice and vodka go in the glass. Dashes of tabasco and Worchester sauce followed but I was really repulsed when he dropped horseradish in before stirring it up with a fresh sprig of celery.

"So, ask," he growled.

My first question was the same one I'd asked Raf. How'd he known the horn would be among the sale items. Oddly enough, he gave nearly the same answer.

"I know a guy who knows a guy who . . ."

I cut him off there. "Any of these guys have names?"

"They aren't always the same guys, Raven, but the whisper started with a dude who is his batty aunt's caretaker."

I wasn't in the least surprised to find the dude's last name was the same as Raphael's witch's. The dragon didn't know his address, but arch boy had already supplied that. I jotted the name down like I'd never heard it before.

"Next question," I announced. "When did you notice the horn wasn't in the safe?"

"Last night, of course. When the two angelics showed up then you strolled into the bar, decided I'd better check on it. That's the first I knew it was gone."

"And you just assumed I'd taken it."

"You got a rep, Farrell."

Hadn't thought it was as a thief but go figure.

"So, after you stole it on Thursday, it went in the safe immediately?"

"I wouldn't call it stealing," the dragon insisted. "It was more putting it in protective custody."

"You know what it can do?"

"Yeah," he said. "Round out my collection nicely. It's ancient and it's a gorgeous piece of workmanship."

Didn't sound like he knew it might be over-the-top deadly. Decided I wasn't going to tell him it was, either.

"Anything out of the ordinary happen around here yesterday?" I asked.

"Holiday weekend, sport. It's always busy with the guys escaping from shopping marathons with wives and sweethearts. We lost the wi-fi feed for the televised grid iron games for around an hour but there was a service tech drinking at the bar who volunteered to get it up and running," he admitted.

"Would he have been in the same room the safe is in to do this repair?"

"Sure, he was, but I was with him the whole time," the dragon insisted.

I tapped my pen on my handy-dandy P.I. notepad. "You didn't happen to notice any lost time while in the room with him?"

Golden amphibian eyes narrowed in suspicion. "You implying I don't know a magic user when I'm looking at one?"

"Not in the least. I'm implying that a magic user pulled a fast one on you, Red. Tell me what this helpful customer looked like."

If a health inspector had walked into the bar right then, The Red Dragon would have been written up for not enforcing the no smoking law. No cured tobacco was being abused on the premises, but the proprietor's temper was providing a visible bit of haze.

The man checking the liquor stock behind the bar glanced at his boss and stepped in to fill the information void. "I was on duty when the sets went black," he said. "The guy who did the repair was about your height, looked like he worked out regularly, had brown hair worn to his shoulders, hadn't shaved in a couple days. Seemed like an outdoors type 'cause he had a natural tan, and his fingertips looked callused. Was wearing a Lions sweatshirt and drinking craft beer. Bell's Black Note Stout."

"You note the color of his eyes?" I asked.

"Naw. I notice what's going to help me serve the correct refill on what a man's drinkin'," he said.

"He have an accent?"

"Sounded just like you or me, buddy," the bartender said.

I turned to the dragon. "You got anything to add to that, Red?"

"Just find him, Raven," my host growled. A bit more smoke entered the air, but I didn't have to stay around to inhale it. I left.

~ ~ ~

The sexy female voice of the GPS's computer guided me from The Red Dragon into a pleasant residential nook far from any part of town I'd visited in the four weeks I'd been on this side of the book binding. The homes were probably less than a decade old, but they were big, proving that not all of Detroit had gotten flushed down the financial drain. They were all two-storied, some with gables that indicated the attics were not just for storage but livable spaces. Three car garages were common. The landscape of each was customized. What vehicles sat in driveways were either family sized or sleek sports cars. As I was still driving the classic 1969 British Racing Green MGB Roadster from my creator's collection of antique cars, my transportation fit right in.

Raphael's witch and the dragon's guy in the know shared quarters with a mid-forties' female, two teenagers and a mutt. Okay, a mutt who probably had AKC ancestors. The dog met me first, got a whiff of Beelz from my pant legs and backed off. A pushing fifty guy with a paunch and a baseball cap turned bill first was hacking at a shrub. The woman was fussing with pots of mums that were determined to call it a year. The teens were heard more than seen, as was the bounce of a basketball in the rear yard.

I parked on the street. The homeowners looked up.

"Hi!" I greeted as I got out of the car. "The name's Farrell. I'm from the Raphael Foundation, sent to visit..." I glanced down at the clipboard in my hand. Yeah, I'd made a quick trip home to run off some fake documents, business cards, and a name tag to pin to the pullover sweater I'd swung by Target to get. It said "trustworthy citizen" more than my abused leather jacket did. "...Clarissa Ponce. Is she feeling up to some company today?"

The man lowered the nasty looking limb decapitator in his hands. "Usually someone calls before coming to see my aunt," he said.

I consulted the clipboard. "They didn't get in touch with you? My sheet has that checked off. I wonder if they called the wrong number."

Apparently unconcerned that it wasn't a good idea to do so, the woman rattled off their contact info. I pulled a pen out and made a note. "They had two numbers reversed. Darn. I suppose I'll need to arrange another visit, unless it's convenient to see Ms. Ponce. If not, no problem."

They exchanged a look. "If she has someone new to talk to, perhaps it will tire her out earlier," the woman said.

The man sighed. "Oh, alright. How long a visit you planning to make?"

"As long as she'd like," I said. "The Raphael Foundation is here to help ease the caregiving burden for families."

"I don't believe I've ever heard of your organization before," the woman admitted.

I smiled. "I get that a lot. The name changed recently but someone from our office has been here before, it just wasn't me. I'm new to this schedule. Be glad to show you my identification."

As I'd run it off the printer less than an hour before, it was quite up to date. The only lie on it was that my first name was Abraham rather than Bram. There weren't many people who knew how to read in the Detroit area – at least that I'd run into – who didn't know Bram Farrell was a fictional character. I wasn't taking chances.

The woman pulled her gardening gloves off as her husband looked at my newly laminated Raphael Foundation ID card. It had a picture and everything. "Do you mind taking Mr. Farrell up," he asked her.

"Of course not. You know she'll want tea to serve so I'll need to make a pot." She sounded resigned. My visit was making work she wasn't happy doing. Sad that she felt that way. "I'll take you up, Mr. Farrell."

She led the way towards a staircase fitted with one of those moving chairs for the handicapped, only the chair seat was tucked up out of the way. "I don't want you to think we're cruel, but Aunt Rissy insisted upon having the third floor rather than the suite we installed for her on the main level. It's a bit of a haul."

"No problem at all," I assured her. Heck, in bad weather I ran from the cellars to the attic back at the Amberson mansion to stay in shape to outdistance anything that might decide to chase me.

"Oh, I should also warn you that she burns incense," Mrs. Ponce said. She wrinkled her nose a bit in disapproval.

I'd already caught a sniff. Sandalwood. And a hint of marijuana. Someone wanted to keep Aunt Rissy calm, happy, and sedated. I wondered whether there would be brownies with the tea when it arrived. Depending on how calm auntie was, I might end up with the munchies.

The staircase to the attic area also was fitted with a handicapped chair devise but it led directly into a wide-open area that was furnished in loft fashion. A couple token walls around what was obviously a bath, a hospital bed nearby, and a cozy living area with upholstered chairs rather than a sofa. The chairs were arranged to face a 50-inch flat screen. Ms. Ponce was watching one of the shopping channels.

She turned to glance at us as we cleared the top step, a grin on her wizened face. Once her niece-in-law introduced me she shooed the woman away with a request for a pot of tea.

"I knew you'd find me," she said.

"*Find* you, Ms. Ponce?" It seemed odd phrasing.

Her grin widened. She leaned on the arm of her chair. "Very clever of you to pretend to be from one of those care groups, Raven."

I'll admit, I started when she used my moniker.

"Why the surprise? I'm a seer."

"I had heard that," I admitted. "But I'm not..."

She raised her hand, forefinger pointing heavenwards. "Know who you are and why you're here. It's very important. There is a horn, a very dangerous horn. It needs to be destroyed."

My mouth probably dropped open.

"Shh," she cautioned. "Just talk visitation garbage until the tea gets here, then we can discuss business."

When the niece returned, Clarissa Ponce and I were debating the color choices available on the Isaac Mizrahi fashion flats the TV host was pushing.

The moment the echo of the front door closing behind the woman reached us, Raphael's seer lost interest in footwear.

"Would you mind lighting us up, Raven?" she asked, nodding at the incense sticks poking from a holder on the table between us.

To make her happy, I did so with a thought rather than a lighter. Her grin was all that I expected but the neatly rolled joint that materialized from her pocket was unexpected. I lit it the same way when she put it to her lips. She drew deeply on it and offered me a hit. I abstained.

"The horn," I said.

"End of days," she corrected and inhaled another cloud of Maryjane. "I'm not ready for the world to end and my spirit friends aren't either. It would lead to serious overcrowding in their realm."

"I can imagine," I sympathized.

"Plus, the only real fun I have these days is irritating my nephew's family." She leaned toward me. "They can't get rid of me. I own the house. Before the horn showed up on my scope, I knew I'd make it to 123. I'm just 87 now, so plenty of time to enjoy myself yet. But not if the damn world ends. That would be a real bummer."

I totally agreed with that.

"So, you've got to destroy it," she said.

"How? I don't even know who's got the damn thing. It went missing again last night."

"Oh, it'll turn up," she assured.

"Any idea when or where?" I might need to make travel plans to be in the right place at the right time, though how the hell I was going to destroy the damn thing was eluding me. Heck, it might not even look like a trombone any longer.

Clarissa stared into the smoke rising from the joss sticks then took another hit on her joint. Her eyes lost clarity as she looked into what I guessed – hoped – was the future. If I was lucky there would be latitude and longitude readings plus Greenwich mean time to the second supplied.

As a long shot, it didn't materialize.

"Oh, it will find you," Clarissa said. "It will appear in the air and you must act quickly, Raven. Others will be there to stop you for they don't know the danger."

"Any particular date or time, Ms. Ponce?"

Her eyes lost that otherworld glaze and refocused on me. "Oh, you can call me Rissy, Raven. Once you destroy the horn, I hope you'll visit again. I don't see many folks with enhanced talents, just the norms."

"I thought an angel visited you regularly. At least he told me he came by," I said.

She wrinkled her nose. "Yeah, he does, but between you and me he's got a bit of a stick up his you-know."

From my own interactions with Raphael, I totally agreed with her.

"The horn will come to me, huh?" I knew I didn't sound happy about that. "Any idea of when?"

"I'll let you know," she said, "but you'll need to act fast when it happens."

"Anything else you can tell me?" I asked.

Rissy chuckled. "You'll do fine," she insisted. "And don't worry about that wish of yours. It'll come about in time. You just have to earn it."

I had a lot of wishes hanging ten, but I'd been around enough seers in fictionland to know clarification wasn't going to be forthcoming.

Neither of us had downed the tea yet. To make the niece-in-law feel appreciated, I emptied my cup. There hadn't been any brownies or other comestibles served with it.

I got to my feet. "Guess I'd better figure out what I need to do."

"Come tell me all about it if the Apocalypse gets put off?" she requested wistfully.

"Promise," I said. "Your doctor let you have pizza?"

"I'm the only doctor I listen to, though I get dragged to see the so-called professionals," she said. "So, yep, I do eat pizza. Thin crust with the works, 'cept anchovies. How about next Thursday?"

It was encouraging to know she believed we'd all still be here on Thursday. I gave her a kiss on the cheek and headed out. Now all I had to do was figure how to destroy something that had been made in Heaven.

~ ~ ~

Rather than head directly home again, I stopped for tacos and while waiting for them to arrive called the television station and asked for the news department. The reporter who'd covered the harmonica story wasn't available, but they were happy to share the address of the mega store where the incident had taken place. They bought the story about me being a freelance writer working on a holiday themed human-interest article. I told them I was collecting odd stories of Salvation Army volunteers' experiences.

Unfortunately, when I got to the store, the guy who'd played the harmonica wasn't on the schedule. But the store had greeters stationed to direct people toward whatever was on their list. That guy had witnessed the harmonica episode and the fellow he described sounded like the same guy who'd fixed the cable feed at The Red Dragon earlier the same day.

Just what I needed. Another mysterious guy to track down. One that might be a demon because, if indeed time had been stopped in the dragon's office, the harmonica owning TV fixer might be a demon. I'd met a demon who could move normally inside a time bubble of their own creation my first day in the real world. To say I was happy to learn there might be another one abroad would be a super-sized fib.

Beelz and I had surprise turkey sandwiches delivered to the door by a harassed looking member from my creator's old coven. A double surprise, as we didn't know she'd be by and after she left found the leftovers were too creative for our palates. Who puts Brie rather than Swiss cheese on a sandwich much less add pecans and arugula? I didn't mind the sourdough bread, but iceberg lettuce and glops of mayo would have suited me better. Fortunately, the only other vegetables that made an appearance were barbecue flavored potato chips from the cupboard and dill pickles from the fridge. Dinner conversation revolved around my limited magical repertoire.

Back in fictionland, I'd been able to do all kinds of things. On this side, I had four things I could do: set things aflame with regular or hellfire, toss balls of either kind of fire, throw small protection shields in place, and send a blast of power that was wind-like but dissipated faster than a sneeze. Not exactly tools for heavenly horn destruction.

Yet, that was my job according to Rissy Ponce. Double jeopardy that I'd be up against two archangels, a dragon, and maybe a mysterious time shaping, harmonica owning demon, none of whom wanted it destroyed.

Which, I realized, might be my ace in the hole. They would think I was just as eager to snag it and keep it as they were. Heck, the time bender might already have it, though from what Rissy had said, maybe not. The horn would come to me, she'd prophesized.

Now all I needed was inspiration for when it did. Maybe fast reflexes, too.

Since there was nothing left to do but wait, I flipped on the big screen. Unfortunately, the news was on. I didn't feel up to dealing with the world's problems, so I switched to a non-news channel and found they were broadcasting the news. As was the all movie channel, every cartoon channel, the porn, cooking, travel, shopping and sports channels plus Netflix, Amazon Prime, Hulu, and the various Spanish language networks. When I hit the weather channel, the commentator was smiling widely at me and pointing to a bright red arrow on the map behind him. It was curving with dead center precision toward Detroit. "Right now, in the Motor City it's a crystal-clear night with a chance of falling horns," he said.

I was up and had thrown the terrace doors wide when I heard Rissy's voice in my head yell, "NOW!" Beelz was still getting to his feet but Sam popped into view on the lawn, his head tilted back to stare up at the stars. The red dragon flashed in next followed by Raphael. We all had our eyes pinned on something that caught a glint of moonlight as it tumbled end over end toward Earth. If it had ever morphed to harmonica, the horn had morphed back. It was a trombone again and gravity was dragging it down fast. The angels and the dragon were in flight immediately, each determined to catch it first. I, of course, couldn't fly.

But they were moving sluggishly. Seemed possible that the time juggler was nearby and intent on aiding me. Since I wasn't affected, I could think faster than any of them were moving. The opportunity wouldn't last long though.

Hoping it would work, I thought an instant encasement of ice into being around the trombone. Not merely artic ice but minus 371-degree Fahrenheit ice, the type found on the coldest place in the solar system. Uranus ice. It had barely formed when I threw a further command. "Shatter!" I yelled. Well, maybe it was a shriek. I was a bit on edge.

I'm not sure which of the three flyers was closest when the trombone turned to un-Earthly cold pixie dust, but all three flinched at the destruction. A nanosecond later, they'd all blipped out of sight, though not before I heard a growl. I think Raf snarled it.

I collapsed on the top step of the terraced path from patio to lawn. Microscopic bits of magic floated down around me. Beelz plopped himself down next to me, resting his muzzle on my thigh, to watch it as well.

"Damn," I breathed. "I think I did it."

"A job well done," a voice I didn't recognize said in the dark, then a being with broad shoulders, shoulder length hair, and a Detroit Lions sweatshirt sat down next to me. He offered a hand. "Name's Gabe," he said by way of introduction.

In reflex, I shook his hand. "Short for Gabriel of the Heavenly Choir?"

"Sometimes," he murmured.

"You couldn't destroy the frickin' thing yourself?"

"Nope. Had to be someone who had no ties to the factions involved."

I sighed. "Well, we certainly had plenty represented. Heaven, Hell, and the world of legends. Some might say I fit in that last one, you know."

"They'd be wrong. You're the only fictional being on the planet. All you wanted was to insure everyone had a future. The others, not so much," Gabe said.

"Even your brothers?"

He chuckled. "Particularly my brothers, Raven. The dragon is simply typical of his kind. He collects shiny, precious objects."

I leaned back on my elbows and stared up into the sky. There were no longer pixie dust sized crystals drifting in the air. Clouds were rushing in to cloak the moon. If they'd arrived sooner, I wouldn't have been able to see the horn tumbling, though Sam, Raf and the dragon would have. There would have been a mighty clash of wings as all three collided and fought over possession of the instrument in midair.

"You corralled them in space-time, didn't you," I said.

Gabriel shrugged. "Playing field needed leveling. I didn't whisper a solution to you when it came to destroying the horn though. That was pure Bram Farrell and an impressively imaginative solution at that."

"What about that trick you played on the dragon, time blipping him to release the horn from his safe? He didn't even realize you were an immortal."

"I have a few tricks to keep my origins unknown," Gabriel admitted. "The horn wasn't supposed to attract quite as much attention as it did, but I didn't tinker with the safe. I just asked the horn to come forth while the world was between seconds."

Who would have thought an instrument capable of ending the world *and* provide a soundtrack while doing so, could pull a Houdini-like escape?

I wasn't quite out of questions for him yet. "Does this mean the Apocalypse is off the books?"

"Wish I could say it was, but it probably isn't. Mankind can bring an end to things without Heavenly intervention these days. In the first century when John of Patmos wrote *Revelations*, he couldn't conceive of the ways men could decimate the planet and beyond, so he wrote what people of the time would take as truth," Gabriel explained. "As you well know, words are both powerful and magical things. They created the horn. I've been trying to figure out a way to take it out of contention for centuries. When you crossed from the page, I knew you were the answer for which I'd prayed."

It was my turn to laugh. "The Raven as an answer to a prayer? I doubt many would see me in that sort of light, Gabe."

"It only takes one believing in you," he said.

"As you believed in the volunteer who knew how to play a harmonica?"

"It worked, didn't it?"

"It confused the frack out of me," I confessed. "I hate red herrings, and that little performance was a heck of one."

"No, just a sideline, Raven. I've been orchestrating things so that nothing pointed back to me from the beginning." He offered his hand. "Thank you for taking care of the horn. I've already given you a more substantial reward than mere words."

"As in an anonymous donation to the bank account?"

Gabe's lips curved in amusement. "Something better. Rissy Ponce. Though it didn't seem like my hand was in the mix, I was the one who lead to your meeting her. Rissy is going to be very helpful to you in the future."

"How?"

But it was too late. He'd skipped out as smoothly as he'd slipped in.

Beelz shifted position. Using my torso as a ramp, he went nose to nose with me then washed my face with his tongue. I wrestled him away so that we could both stare at the night sky. When it started to snow, all seemed quite right with the world once more.

RAVEN'S REWARD

At least temporarily. Who knows what dawn would bring.

RAVEN'S REWARD

Feed an Author

Leave a Review! Tell us what you liked!

Appreciate it!

For more Raven Tales adventures
look for either the novels,
Raven's Moon and *Marked Raven*
or snag one of the prequels.

About the Author:

J.B. DANE is a pseudonym of a multi-published, multi-genre novelist who goes by many names. Not because she is in Witness Protection. Really not in Witness Protection. Really. She may start hiding from citizens of Detroit since her Raven Tales urban fantasy comedic mysteries have populated their fair city with neighbors who might be supernatural, paranormal, or legendary beasts . . . or not so beasts . . . but probably ARE beasts. They could be hungry, too. She dabbles with other tales of comedic fantasy and has tampered with the lore of the Claus family, you know the one at the North Pole, and hopes this does not land her on the Naughty List, even if Nick Claus *has* landed on it frequently himself.

She *might* be found at
www.4TaleTellers.com
but leave a message to be picked up
by a disguised courier and delivered
to a secret location.
Ditto via Facebook.com/JBDaneWriter
or @JBDaneWriter on Twitter

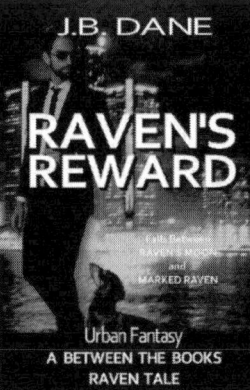

Bram and Beelz are Back!

**Don't miss the Prequels
Bram's cases back in fictionland**

Made in the USA
Columbia, SC
29 January 2021